Tommy the Throwaway Dog

Written by Laura Marlowe
Illustrated by Javier Duarte

ISBN 978-1-936352-51-7
1-936352-51-6

Published by Mirror Publishing
Milwaukee, WI 53214

Printed in the USA.

This story is dedicated to the kind staff of Horseshoe Lake Animal Hospital, Collinsville, IL; Hope Rescues Animal Shelter, Alton, IL; The Cahokia, IL Police Department; every person who cared enough to give Tommy a second chance; and Tommy, the bravest dog ever.

One autumn day when the colored leaves were falling and the air was turning chilly, a trash collector was on his usual rounds when he discovered a black dog inside a trash can.

The dog was covered in a big pile of trash. It seemed as though someone had simply thrown the dog away. The man noticed that the dog had no collar. He did not see any tags anywhere either.

The dog was very, very scared. And very, very hurt. And very, very sad. He looked at the man, and the man looked at him. The kind man called the police right away.

When the policeman arrived, he carefully took the dog out of the trash can and brushed away the mess and the dirt.

He was very saddened by what he saw. The dog started to shake with fear. The kind policeman felt bad for the dog.

After a few minutes, the dog surprised the policeman by wagging his tail.

Then, he stopped shaking.
The policeman took some photographs, gently put the dog into his police car, and took him to the veterinarian.

The kind veterinarian examined the dog. The dog needed a lot of care, including medicine, surgery, and rest. He had been badly hurt.

Still, the dog wagged his tail. The veterinarian smiled at the dog and patted him on the head.

After his time in the animal hospital, the dog was taken to the animal shelter.

The kind shelter people gave him a bed, some toys, a lot of hugs, and a lot of good food and vitamins.

All these things were new to him. He did not know what to do with them or think about them, so he just stared. Yet, to the delight of the shelter staff, the dog wagged his tail.

The shelter people named him Tommy, the throwaway dog.

Meanwhile, a kind person who knew the owner of the dog found out what happened and went to the police to file a report. Soon after, the mean person who hurt Tommy was arrested and put in jail. Many people were happy to see justice served.

The shelter people continued to work very hard to care for Tommy.

Every day, he got better and better. He ate his food, learned how to play with all the toys, and enjoyed seeing everyone at the shelter.

He ran in the small backyard and chased after things. He loved to play.

He was even happy when he had to go to the veterinarian for check-ups. He wagged his tail.

As time went on, the shelter needed money to help support Tommy's care. They asked for donations, and soon afterward, the shelter started to receive money, food, and toys from many kind people.

Some even called or wrote letters asking about Tommy.

Eventually, there were requests to adopt him.

One day, Tommy was offered a new home with a special family who would love him and help him forget all about the scary time.

The shelter people would miss him very much, but they knew that it was time to say goodbye and that Tommy would be happy to finally have a real home.

Everyone at the shelter was thankful and promised to visit Tommy whenever they could.

When Tommy found out he had a new home, Tommy wagged his tail.
And he hasn't stopped wagging his tail ever since.

CPSIA information can be obtained at www.ICGtesting.com
Printed in the USA
LVIW01n1923220415
435661LV00009B/21